Maude and Sally

and Sally

PUFFIN BOOKS

I think we're supposed to go this way, Sally

PUFFIN BOOKS
Viking Penguin Inc., 40 West 23rd Street,
New York, New York 10010, U.S.A.
Penguin Books Ltd, 27 Wrights Lane, London W8 5TZ
(Publishing & Editorial), and Harmondsworth,
Middlesex, England (Distribution & Warehouse)
Penguin Books Australia Ltd, Ringwood,
Victoria, Australia
Penguin Books Canada Limited, 2801 John Street,
Markham, Ontario, Canada L3R 1B4
Penguin Books (N.Z.) Ltd, 182–190 Wairau Road,
Auckland 10, New Zealand

First Published by Greenwillow Books, 1983
Published in Picture Puffins 1988
By arrangement with William Morrow and Company, Inc.
Copyright © Monica J. Weiss, 1983
All rights reserved
Printed in Japan by Dai Nippon Printing Co. Ltd.
Set in Lubalin Graph Book

Library of Congress Cataloging-in-Publication Data
Weiss, Nicki.   Maude and Sally / Nicki Weiss.
p.   cm.
Summary: When her best friend Sally goes to summer camp, Maude
finds she can become best friends with Emmylou also.
ISBN 0-14-050760-4
(1. Friendship—Fiction.) I. Title.
(PZ7.W448145Mau 1988)   (E)—dc19   87-20911

FOR PEGGY

Maude and Sally were best friends.
And as far as Maude was concerned,
it was a perfect match.

"If you were a little taller and I was a little shorter," Maude would say,
"we could be twins."

Sally and Maude would meet
at the corner of Dupont and Gedney
and walk to school.

At lunch they traded sandwiches.
"Bologna and cream cheese today,"
Maude would say,
as Sally would hand over half
a peanut butter and jelly.

In gym Maude picked Sally for her softball team, even though Sally usually missed the ball.

And for spelling bee, Sally picked Maude to be on her team, even though Maude thought you spelled "TOUGH" with an "F".

If Emmylou sat between them in the music room, they made her change places.

And in their homeroom they pushed their desks so close together that no one could pass through the aisle.

"I'll have to separate you two if you can't stop whispering," Mrs. O'Brien would say.

After school they played dress-up,
and sometimes
Maude let Sally wear
the green satin high heels.

(Maude had to wear
the black-and-white ones
that looked like saddle shoes.)

Some afternoons
they made phoney phone calls
in a foreign accent to Simon,
who lived across the street from Maude.

And most Friday nights
Maude asked her mother
if Sally could sleep over,
or if she could sleep
at Sally's.

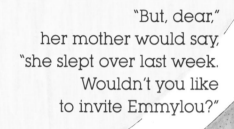

"But, dear,"
her mother would say,
"she slept over last week.
Wouldn't you like
to invite Emmylou?"

"If your hair was a little shorter
and mine was a little longer,"
Maude would say to Sally
once they were under the covers,
"we could be twins."

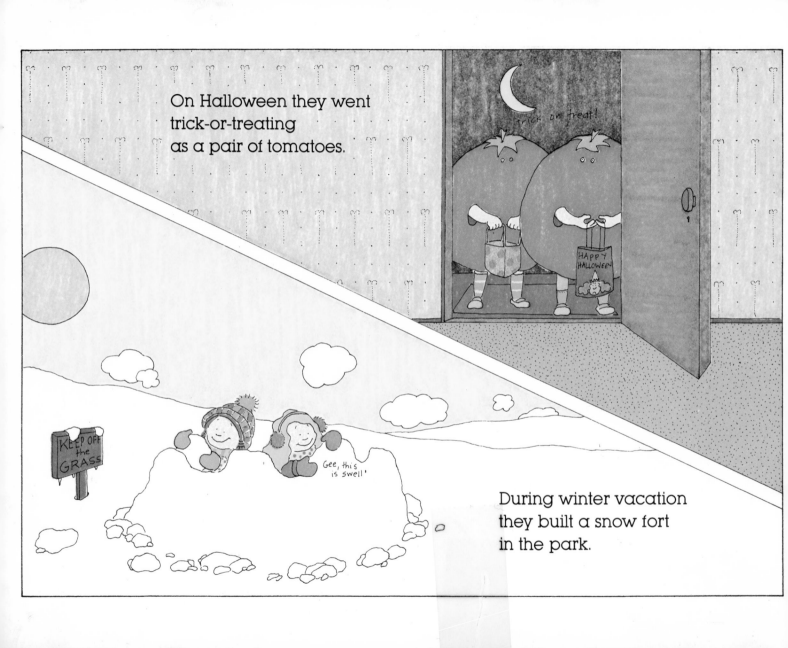

On Halloween they went
trick-or-treating
as a pair of tomatoes.

During winter vacation
they built a snow fort
in the park.

And, although neither of them got the part of Cinderella in the spring play,

they were big hits as Cinderella's two stepsisters.

And then it was summer, and Sally was going to camp.
"If I was going, too," Maude said,
"I'd share a bunk bed with you."

"It's only for six weeks, Maude,"
Sally said, and then she was off.

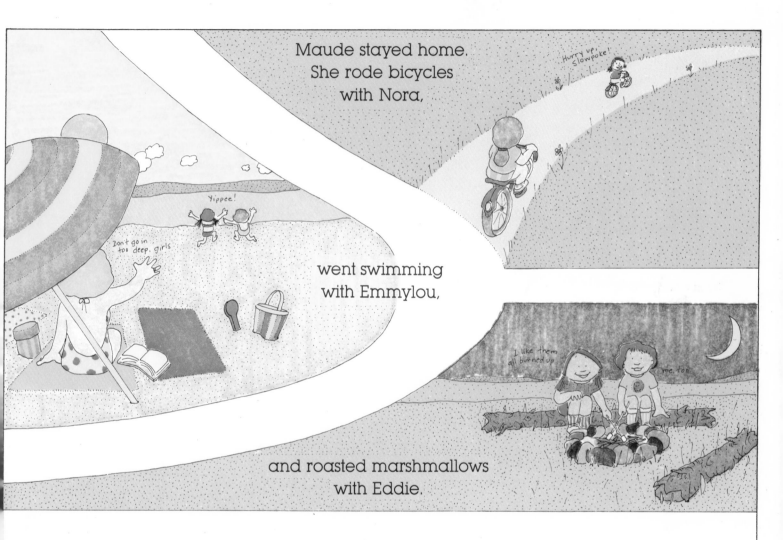

Maude stayed home.
She rode bicycles
with Nora,

went swimming
with Emmylou,

and roasted marshmallows
with Eddie.

But every day she waited for a letter from Sally.

Then she hardly wrote at all.

"Maude, dear," Mama said, "Sally will be home soon. She's just so busy with all sorts of new things. Why don't you invite someone else to sleep over?"

"But it won't be the same," said Maude.

When Emmylou came
with her sleeping bag
the next afternoon, Maude said,
"You wear the black-and-white high heels."

When they sat at the piano,
and Emmylou didn't know
how to play chopsticks, Maude said,
"Everyone in the world knows how to play that."

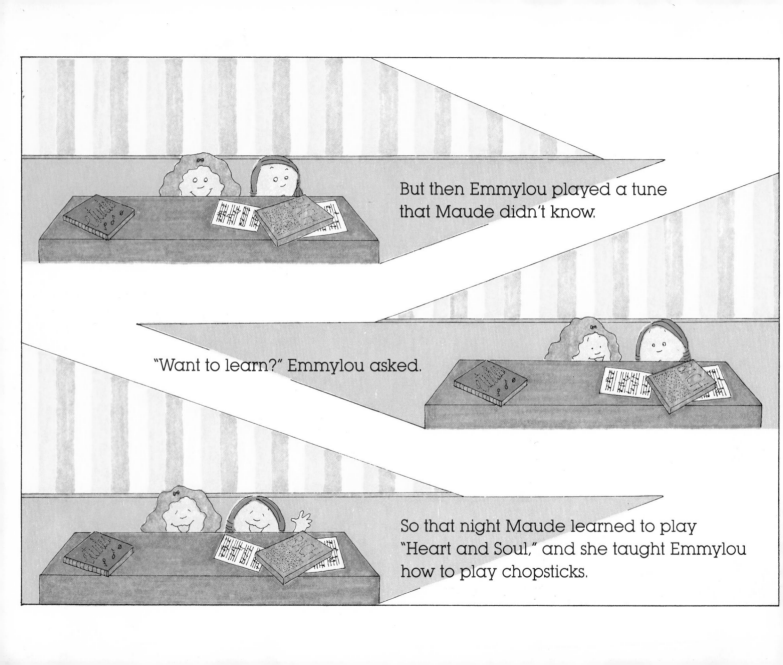

But then Emmylou played a tune
that Maude didn't know.

"Want to learn?" Emmylou asked.

So that night Maude learned to play
"Heart and Soul," and she taught Emmylou
how to play chopsticks.

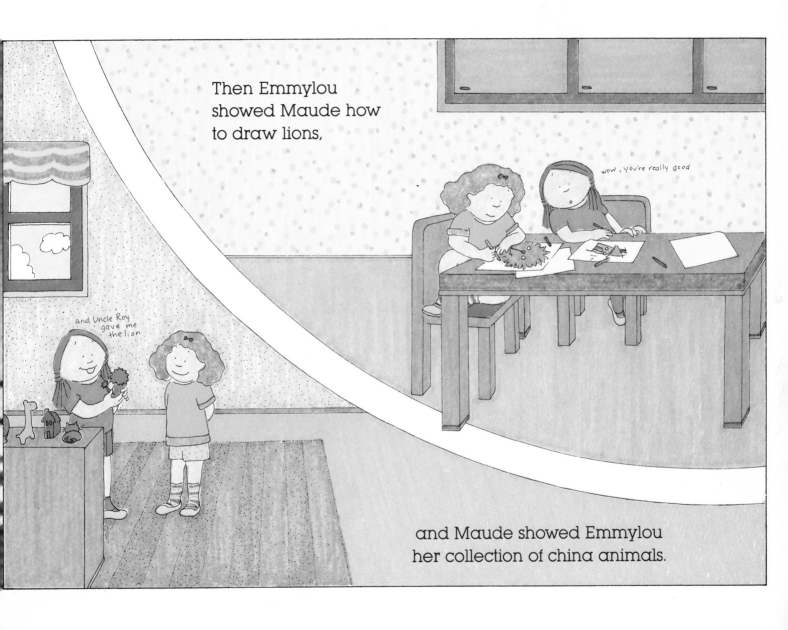

Then Emmylou
showed Maude how
to draw lions,

wow, you're really good

and Uncle Roy
gave me
the lion

and Maude showed Emmylou
her collection of china animals.

They played hide-and-seek.

They sneaked a few more cookies into their pockets before they went to bed.

And when the lights were out,
they told each other scary stories until they fell asleep.

The weeks passed, summer was almost over, and Sally came home from camp.

She showed Maude her pictures of the canoe trip, of the campfires, and of the girl who shared her bunk bed.

Then school began, and
once again the two girls met
at the corner of Dupont and Gedney.

They walked to school together
and traded sandwiches at lunchtime.

"Tunafish and cucumbers,"
Maude would say
as Sally would give her
half a salami on rye.

But now when they went to the music room,
Emmylou sat on one side of Maude
while Sally sat on the other.

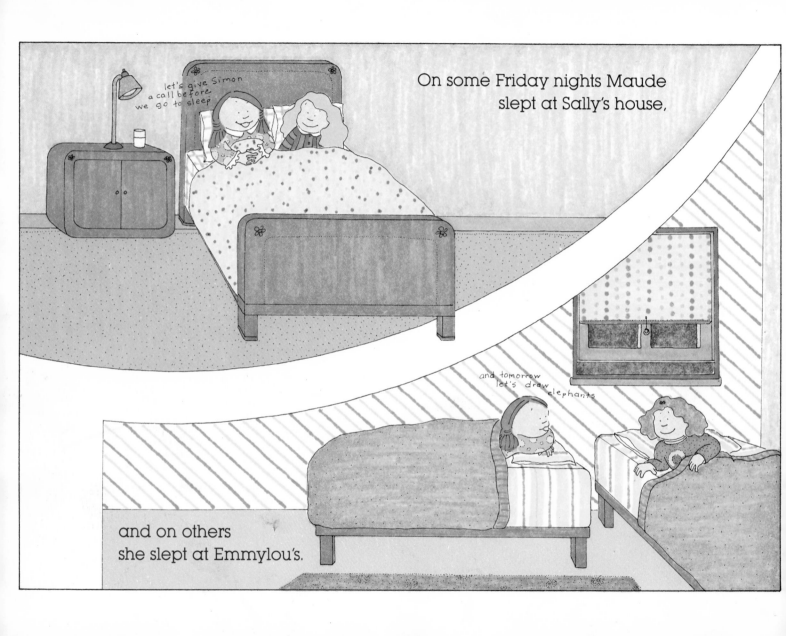

On some Friday nights Maude
slept at Sally's house,

and on others
she slept at Emmylou's.

And on Halloween Maude and Sally and Emmylou dressed up as bumblebees.

"If your wings were a little bigger," Maude said to Emmylou, "and your antennae were a little longer," she said to Sally,

"we could be triplets."

I think I'll pick some daisies for Maude

I think I'll pick some daisies for Emmylou

I think I'll pick some daisies for Sally